For my mum, who looks after
my park when I am away. ~ A.

For my amma Birgitta who always
waited by the window for me.
I miss you and carry you always
in my heart. ~ B.S.

First published 2020 by Walker Books Ltd, 87 Vauxhall Walk, London SE11 5HJ • Text © 2020 Atinuke • Illustrations © 2020 Birgitta Sif • The rights of Atinuke and Birgitta Sif to be identified as author and illustrator respectively of this work have been asserted by them in accordance with the Copyright, Designs and Patents Act 1988 • This book has been typeset in Architype Regular • Printed in China • All rights reserved. No part of this book may be reproduced, transmitted or stored in an information retrieval system in any form or by any means, graphic, electronic or mechanical, including photocopying, taping and recording, without prior written permission from the publisher. • British Library Cataloguing in Publication Data: a catalogue record for this book is available from the British Library • ISBN 978-1-4063-7929-7 • www.walker.co.uk • 10 9 8 7 6 5 4 3 2 1

HUGO

Written by **Atinuke**

Illustrated by **Birgitta Sif**

WALKER BOOKS

AND SUBSIDIARIES

LONDON • BOSTON • SYDNEY • AUCKLAND

My name is Hugo.
I am a park warden.
I look after the park
and I look after the people
who live around it.
It is my job.

In the Spring
I encourage Monsieur
Petit to take his walk.

I keep Madame
Grande company
as she takes the sun.

I discuss the news with Monsieur Occupé.

In the Summer
I do my best to clean up...

after Minou

and Chérie and Puce

and all their friends and relations.

In the Autumn I help to exercise Bébé
and Coquine so their mothers can rest.

And in the Winter
I visit everybody.
I remind them that
Spring will not be long.

But there is one window
where the curtains are never open.
I still visit. I knock politely.
I see somebody hide whenever
she hears a sound.

Then one day
I see Somebody!

I do my
Spring-is-coming
dance and Somebody
smiles a little smile.

Now every day Somebody is waiting.
Waiting to hear me knock.
Waiting to see me dance.

Until the day that I am late...

and Somebody opens the window!
Somebody leans out to look for me!

I am so happy
I do a showing-off
dance on the bench.

I do not see the dog . . .

until it is too late!

Somebody cries,

"Non!"

When I wake up my wing hurts.
I do not want to hop.
I know I cannot fly.

Somebody brings
me water.

Somebody brings
me crumbs.

Somebody strokes
my wing.

Then one day I can!
I can hop, hop, hop!
Somebody laughs and
claps for me!

I hop to the window.
I knock politely.
Somebody shakes
her head.

I knock again.
And again.

Somebody looks so sad.
She wants me to stay
here with her.

But I knock and knock and knock
until Somebody opens the window for me.
She does not want me to be sad,
so she has to let me go.

I hop onto the window sill
and flutter to the ground.

I hop and hop towards the bench.
It takes a long, long time.

I am so tired I rest my beak
on the ground.

Monsieur Petit, Madame Grande,
Monsieur Occupé, Minou,
Chérie, Puce, Bébé and Coquine
all come to their windows and cheer
and cheer and cheer me on!

I flutter to the park bench
to do my little dance.

"*Non!*" Somebody cries.

But it is only Monsieur Petit's dog.
He is my old friend.

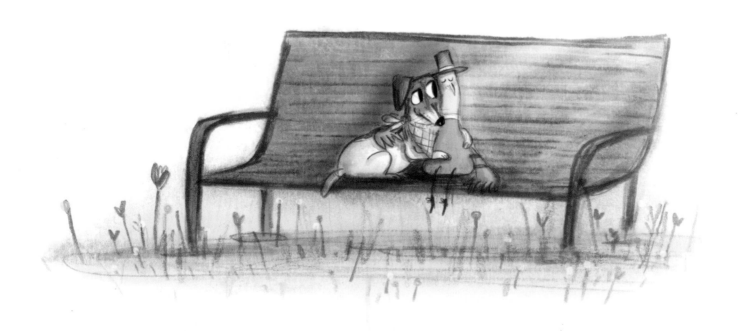

But who is this running to save me?

Does she want to play?

I cock my head.
Somebody smiles!

Up and down and up and down

and up and down we go ...

until Somebody is laughing…

And all the children run out
to play with her.

"Aimée!"
her mother shouts.

And all the children join in,
"Aimée! Aimée! Aimée!"

My name is Hugo.

I am a park warden.
I look after the park
and I look after the people
who live here.
It is my job.

I love my job!